My Big Brother Troy

Written By
Danielle Wallace
With
Mario Dewberry
Illustrated By
Jeff Purnawan

To Betty Lois Hagger.
My yellow rose.

Being a little sister can be so exhausting, but when you have a cool big brother like Troy, it can be really fun.

We do everything together. We play.
We laugh. We dance. We laugh more.
We watch movies. We scream to see
who can get the loudest.

We run....
And run...
And run...
And run!

We're almost just alike!

But mom and dad said my brother is a little different. Troy is unique in his own way and sometimes that means we have to be more patient.

I have 2 eyes and so does my brother. I have 2 hands, 2 feet, 10 fingers and 10 toes... so does my brother. And we like the same things! How are we different?

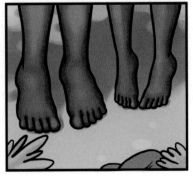

Mom and dad said being different isn't always something we see. They said my brother is different because he doesn't learn like kids his age and some people don't understand him.

They called it being *developmentally delayed.*

But I don't know what that means... I wonder if that's like saying he's funny because he always makes me laugh. Or saying he's nice because he gives the best hugs. Is that like saying he smells funny?
He is a boy after all!

Sometimes he gets really
excited and doesn't say what
makes him so happy. So he
laughs and laughs and
laughs!

So I laugh too!
(And I always see
mom and dad smile!)

Mom and dad worry about my brother Troy a lot, but I think they just need me to remind them of how "alike" we are. He may not know how to say all of the words to express what he thinks or tell how he feels, but if we just pay attention, it's always clear.

When my brother Troy doesn't know how to say the words to ask for what he wants, he cries because he feels like no one is listening. So we both cry until mom and dad figure it out.

When he is upset and feels like no one can understand him, he screams really loud. Since I'm the little sister, I have to do my job. So, I scream too!

But when we do that, mom and dad get upset too. We need them to be more patient, but that will never happen if *EVERYBODY* *gets upset.*

My work as a little
sister is *NEVER* done!

Sometimes I want to cuddle with mom and dad all by myself. I curl up to dad while he's watching tv and just when I think it's only me, dad and basketball, my brother takes over my space.

And sometimes when I'm playing all by myself, my brother takes the toys.

One time I was playing with my blocks. I was building the tallest tower anyone's ever built and when I only had one more block to go, Troy knocked everything down. I was so upset, I screamed loud enough for the whole world to hear.

When mom and dad finally calmed me down a little and I went back to find the blocks, my brother Troy was rebuilding the tower!

"Oh no, Sis!" said Troy, "I fix it."

My brother Troy is not perfect, but neither am I and neither are you. As I continued to think about what all of our differences could be, I thought what if everything I can say with words, some people can show with actions.

As I calmed down, I thought he may not know how to say all of the words to express what he thinks or tell how he feels, but if we just pay attention, it's always clear. If we're patient with him, we'll learn and we'll understand.

"Thanks Troy, I love you too... and don't worry, I'm still working on mom and dad, but we have a little more work to do."

ABOUT THE AUTHOR

As a product of Detroit Public Schools and a graduate of Michigan State University with a Bachelors of Arts in Education, Danielle Wallace is a children's book author with hopes of giving a voice to underrepresented communities. She is a graduate student studying at Eastern Michigan University, as well as a member of the Society of Children's Book Writers and Illustrators. Additionally, she is a freelance writer for The Blasting News online publication. Upon completing her undergraduate degree in education and entering the work field, she has worked to design and facilitate youth programs and staff professional development workshops targeted toward enhancing cultural competence/proficiency and aimed at students who may need individualized attention. She has also worked in areas of community and family engagement, bridging communities, families and schools.